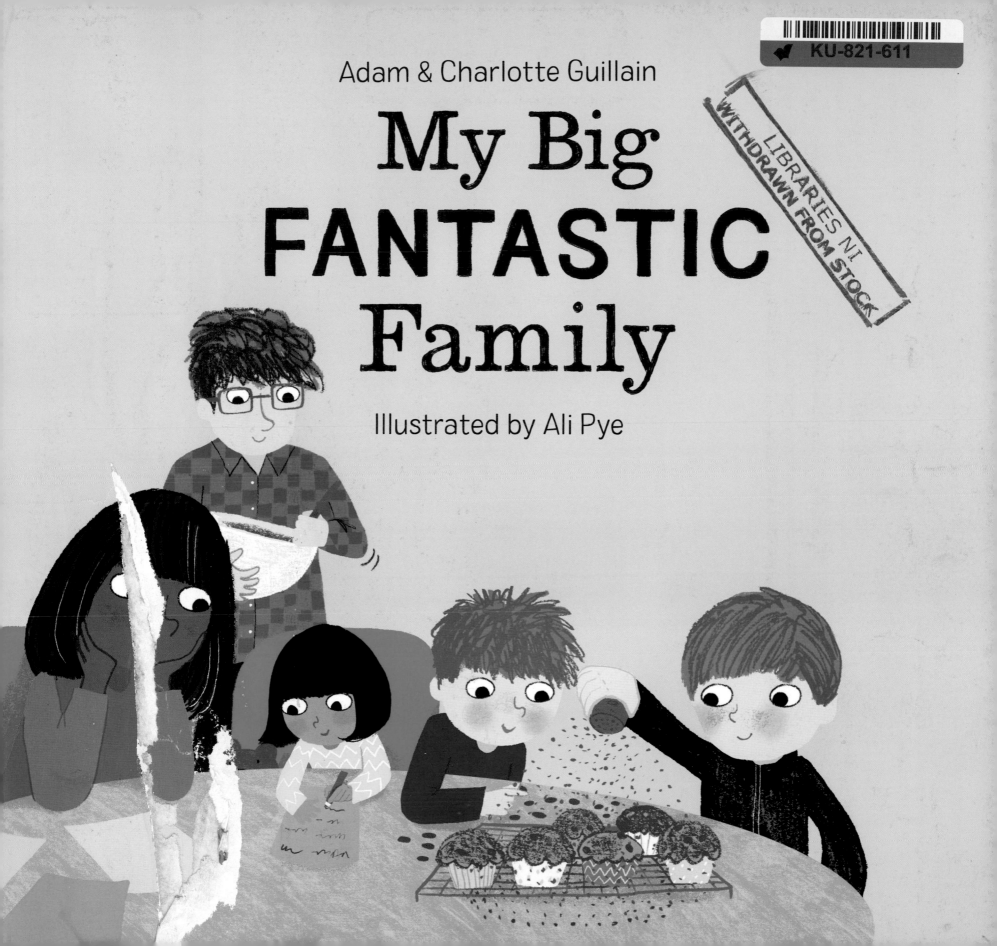

Adam & Charlotte Guillain

My Big FANTASTIC Family

Illustrated by Ali Pye

KU-821-611

LIBRARIES NI
WITHDRAWN FROM STOCK

Hello! My name is Lily-May.
I live with Mum, not Dad.

A lot of things have had to change,
and sometimes I feel sad.

When Mum and Dad first told me
Dad was going to move away,
I hugged Blue Bear and shouted, "No!"
I wanted Dad to stay.

I felt all upside-down inside,
but they both hugged me tight.

"It's **not** your fault," they said to me,
"It's going to be alright."

So Dad drives down on Sundays now,
and we go out to play.
I **always** take Blue Bear with me
to share our special day.

We **love** to do exciting things,
like riding super fast.
We race our bikes downhill,
and people gasp as we zoom past!

I play more just with Mum now, too.
We read books all the time.

We make more models out of junk
and play with squidgy slime!

There's more time to make stories up –
more stories mean more fun!

And now my mum's with Peter –
well, there's more of . . .
everyone!

I used to just have Gran, but now
there's Gramps and Granny G.
That's Peter's mum and dad –
they're **great** at playing games with me.

There's Ben now, and there's Theo, too –
they're Peter's older boys.
They come to stay on Saturdays,
and now we have more . . . noise!

But when Mum started working late,
the first time Peter cooked,
I didn't like his spicy sauce
or how the noodles looked.

I wanted Dad to cook for me
the way that I like best . . .

I scrunched my eyes up tight
and felt a thumping in my chest.

I tried to **wish** things back
to when they didn't feel mixed up.

Then Peter made hot chocolate for me
in my special cup.

We read some bedtime stories,
then we sang a funny song.

When Mum came home,
she **hugged** me,
and she laughed and sang along!

Next day, I went to stay with Dad.
I knew it would be great.

My bag was stuffed with toys and books.
I really couldn't wait!

And when at last Mum dropped me off,
I ran inside Dad's flat.
"I've got a **big surprise**," said Dad . . .

"Oh, wow!" I cheered.
"A cat!"

Dad showed me how to feed her,

and she found a place to hide.

I made a secret den with Dad
and **snuggled** up inside.

But later on, when bedtime came,
I brushed my teeth and hair,

then had a really awful thought,
and asked Dad,

"Where's Blue Bear?"

We looked under the duvet,
and my heart began to pound.

We ran around and searched the flat . . .

. . . Blue Bear could **not** be found!

So Dad gave me a cuddle,
and we called Mum on the phone . . .

"I've just tucked Blue Bear in," she said.
"Don't cry – he's not alone."

The next day, when Dad drove me back,
he had a chat with Mum.
We planned my birthday party
and invited . . . everyone!

So me and Mum picked party games,
while Peter baked some cakes.
Then Ben and Theo stuck on sweets,
and sprinkled chocolate flakes!

Then when **at last** the big day came,
I waited by the door.
I thought about how things have changed . . .

. . . and how there's **so much more!**

More people to play party games
and loads more dancing now.
A lot more people laughing
and a lot more presents – WOW!

I say goodbye more often now,
but when it's time to go,
I know goodbye will only last
until our next hello.

I've got more places I belong.
"Where's home?" my friends ask me.
It's **anywhere** I'm with . . .

. . . my **big** fantastic family.